Javi
Takes a
BOW

Elizabeth Gordon

An imprint of Enslow Publishing

WEST **44** BOOKS™

Milo on Wheels   Noah the Con Artist

Javi Takes a Bow   Club Zoe

Addy's Big Splash

Please visit our website, www.west44books.com. For a free color catalog of all our high-quality books, call toll free 1-800-542-2595 or fax 1-877-542-2596.

Cataloging-in-Publication Data
Names: Gordon, Elizabeth.
Title: Javi takes a bow / Elizabeth Gordon.
Description: New York : West 44, 2020. | Series: The club
Identifiers: ISBN 9781538382455 (pbk.) | ISBN 9781538382462 (library bound) | ISBN 9781538383230 (ebook)
Subjects: LCSH: Friendship--Juvenile fiction. | After-school programs--Juvenile fiction. | Musicals--Juvenile fiction. | Auditions--Juvenile fiction. | Courage in children--Juvenile fiction.
Classification: LCC PZ7.G673 Ja 2019 | DDC [E]--dc23

First Edition

Published in 2020 by
Enslow Publishing
111 East 14th Street, Suite 349
New York, NY 10003

Copyright © 2020 Enslow Publishing

Editor: Theresa Emminizer
Designer: Sam DeMartin

Photo Credits: front matter (basketball) LHF Graphics/Shutterstock.com; front matter (planets) Nikolaeva/ Shutterstock.com; front matter, back matter chapter icon (hurricane) GO BANANAS DESIGN STUDIO/ Shutterstock.com; front matter (stickers) U.P.images_vector/Shutterstock.com; front matter (paint splatter) Milan M/ Shutterstock.com; front matter (boomerang) hchjjl/Shutterstock.com; front matter (game strategy) Dejan Popovic/ Shutterstock.com; front matter (broken bone) BlueRingMedia/Shutterstock.com; front matter (Guatemala stamp) astudio/Shutterstock.com; front matter (bandaids) lineartestpilot/Shutterstock.com; front matter (ants) Viktorija Reuta/ Shutterstock.com; front matter (bulletin board) Franzi/Shutterstock.com; chapter titles (music notes) mhatzapa/ Shutterstock.com; p. 3 sinoptic/Shutterstock.com;
p. 4 shamcanggih/Shutterstock.com; p. 9 TheBlackRhino/Shutterstock.com; p. 11 advent/Shutterstock.com; p. 18 LHF Graphics/Shutterstock.com; p. 24 Kamolcha/Shutterstock.com; p. 33 hchjjl/Shutterstock.com; p. 43 ArtMari/ Shutterstock.com; p. 54 Kudryashka/Shutterstock.com; pp. 61, 62 AuraArt/Shutterstock.com; feather icons Watercolor_swallow/Shutterstock.com.

Printed in the United States of America

CPSIA compliance information: Batch #CS18W44: For further information contact
Enslow Publishing, New York, New York at 1-800-542-2595.

the CLUB

Milo Braverman

Most likely to have a toad in his pocket

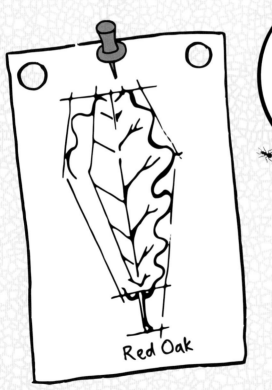

Red Oak

COMEBACK KID

EMBODIMENT
OF TEVYE

Javi Morales

Most likely to know all the words to *Hamilton*

Addy Prescott

Most likely to break an arm playing ping-pong

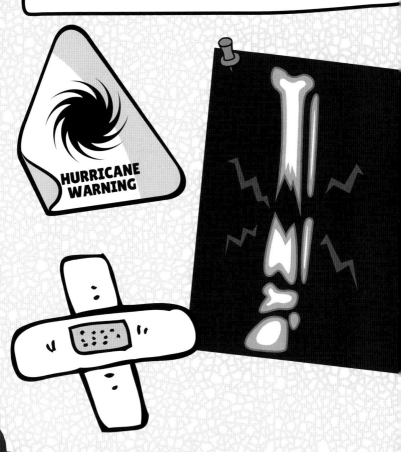

HURRICANE WARNING

Noah Spencer

Most likely to have paint in his hair

RESIDENT ARTIST

Zoe Spencer

Most likely to correct your free throw form

PLAYER OF THE GAME

Chapter One
November

Javi slipped and slid on the icy path. Freezing water seeped into his thin sneakers. He shivered. *Maybe I should stop walking through the park.*

It was November. For two months, Javi had gotten off the city bus one stop early. He liked cutting through the park to his after-school program. There were tall, leafy trees and green meadows. They were a faint reminder of the colorful landscapes of his home.

But now, the park was empty. The sun was already setting. The ground was covered in snow. Trees were brown and bare. A sharp wind found its way through his jacket. And Javi's hometown in the Guatemalan highlands seemed farther away than ever.

It had been four months since Javi had arrived in the United States with his mother, grandmother, and little sister. They were all living in his uncle's apartment. Javi and his sister were in school full-time. They had enough food to eat. What remained of his family was safe. Javi knew he should be grateful. But this new city was like a different planet. Who knew a park could be so silent, cold, and colorless?

Javi pulled his headphones out of his bag. He put them on carefully. He needed them to last. They were held together with tape in a couple of places.

He was even more careful with his cassette player. It was tucked safely in an inner pocket. No amount of money could replace it. Nobody sold them anymore. And anyway, Javi didn't want anything new. This cassette player had belonged to his father.

Javi pressed the play button. The music washed over him. He remembered the last time he'd heard this song with Papá. They had sat close. They had each held an ear to a headphone. They were trying to listen together.

Now, Papá was gone.

Javi didn't want to think about that.

He turned up the volume.

His father had loved American musicals.

This song was from one of them. Javi hadn't understood the English words. Papá had tried to explain the story. It was about a poor family living in a cold place like this one. It had a funny name. *Fiddler on the Roof.* Javi loved the music. It was full of loss and longing. It seemed to fit his mood.

Javi's family used to spend many evenings singing songs from Papá's musicals. Or learning Guatemalan songs and legends from Javi's grandmother, Abuelita. Tevye and Maria von Trapp were familiar friends from the musicals. So was the Mayan hero Tecún Umán. And the quetzal. Javi loved folktales about the rare bird with shimmering green and red feathers. It lived in the cloud forests near their home.

The life Javi and

his family had left behind hadn't been easy. But it had been full of music and stories.

In this new country, Javi's life was mostly silent. It was like this frozen park. There was no singing or storytelling. His uncle and mother worked long hours. His grandmother kept house, but she did not chatter and hum like she used to. Javi often found her sleeping in a chair or staring out a window.

At school, Javi was even more silent. By now, he could understand a lot of things people said. Especially if they didn't talk too fast. But kids laughed at his thick accent when he spoke. So Javi kept to himself. He studied his books. Slowly and painfully, he forced the strange words to make sense to him. It was hard. School had been easy for him in Guatemala. He had been at the top of his class.

Javi started skidding down the last hill. The

Parkside Community Center stood at the bottom. Its after-school program, The Club, was a bright spot in Javi's life. It was the one place outside of his apartment where he would sometimes talk. He'd made a few friends there. The director, Miguel, spoke Spanish. And he was getting help with his schoolwork.

Javi wished his seven-year-old sister Ana would come to The Club. He thought she'd like it. But Ana was afraid. She hadn't been the same since Papá died. Of course, none of them had. But a light had gone out in Ana. Every day after school, she went straight home to their grandmother. She and Abuelita would sit on the couch and watch TV shows they could not understand.

The music swelled to a final chorus. The sweet, sad melody tugged at his heart. His father had said the people in the story were being driven from their village. The song was about leaving everything they knew. *That's like me*, thought Javi. *I wonder if I'll ever feel at home again.*

He pulled open the door of The Club and went in.

Chapter Two
The Announcement

Javi went to The Club's snack area. His friends Milo and Addy were sitting at a table. Milo looked up. "Hi, Javi. Did you find anything today?"

Javi shook his head. "Much cold," he said.

"You mean *very* cold." Addy said. Addy volunteered in the tutoring center. She was helping Javi with his English and his schoolwork.

Milo nodded. "That's okay. I'm still working on this spider. Miguel found it in the janitor's closet." He held up a jar. "*Lycosidae*. Wolf spider.

I'm not sure which species yet."

Addy rolled her eyes. "Milo. I am trying to eat. Could you put that away?"

Javi glanced at the little brown spider trying to scramble up the glass. He spread his hands. "In Guatamala, very bigger."

Addy smiled. "You mean *much* bigger."

Javi sighed. English was impossible.

Milo put the jar on the ground. "I wish I could go to Guatemala," he said. "There must be so much amazing wildlife."

Javi nodded. His father had often taken him up into the cloud forests near his home. There were lots of tree frogs, beetles, and lizards. On one trip, they had spotted a shy, little margay cat. And once, just once, they had seen quetzals.

Milo would love the cloud forest.

Milo loved everything about nature. He had a sketchbook that he called his "Field Guide." He drew pictures of the new plants and creatures he found. He wrote down everything he learned about them.

Javi often helped Milo with his guide. Milo's legs didn't work right. He had to walk with crutches. So Javi found things in the park for Milo. It was a connection to his old life.

Addy finished her snack. She asked, "What homework do you have this weekend, Javi?"

Javi pulled his books out of his bag and handed Addy his planner. She read over his assignments. Meanwhile, Javi got his lunch out of his backpack.

Javi was always starving by the time he got to The Club. He didn't eat much at school. The cafeteria served really strange-looking food. And he didn't like to eat the *empanadas* his grandmother made him while he was there. It would just be another reason for the kids at school to tease him.

He bit into the spicy pastry. Then he pulled out a thermos and took a swig of sweet coffee. Everything was cold by now. But it tasted like home.

His friends at The Club were surprised that he drank coffee. Javi didn't understand it. Even very small children drank coffee in Guatemala.

This sort of thing made him feel tired at the end of every day. There were so many differences. Nothing was normal. The Club was better than most places. But even here, he never felt completely at ease.

Milo put his spider back on the table. He wanted to work on his drawing. Addy made a list of the assignments she and Javi should work on. It was long. Javi pulled his books toward him and got busy.

Miguel came by a few minutes later. Older kids at The Club didn't have to be in activities all the time. As long as they obeyed the rules, Miguel let them hang out. But he checked on everybody every day.

Today, Miguel had a bunch of posters tucked under one big, tattooed arm.

Addy pointed. "What are those, Miguel?"

"Announcements," Miguel said. "For the winter musical."

Javi was usually a couple sentences behind in every conversation. It took time to figure out what people were saying. But musical was a word

Javi definitely knew. It sounded nearly the same in Spanish. He looked up.

"Cool!" said Addy. She tried to see the posters.

Miguel smiled and held them to his chest. "Everyone will find out the name of the musical on Monday. But I hope you'll audition, Addy. We're going to need a violinist. Tryouts are next Friday."

"I don't think you want me to try out, Miguel," Milo said. "I'm tone-deaf."

"What about helping with the tech?" Miguel said. "I need someone to control the light board."

Just then Javi's two other friends walked up to the table. Noah and Zoe were twins. They weren't much alike. Noah spent most of his time in the art room. Zoe was captain of the basketball team. But Javi liked them both a lot.

"Hey, guys!" Addy said. She spun around to talk to them. She knocked into the spider jar as she did so. It spun across the table. Javi caught the jar just before it crashed to the ground.

"Whoops!" said Addy, laughing. "Thanks, Javi."

Javi smiled as he put the jar back on the table. He had learned to be quick around Addy. She was very smart, but she was also *torpe*, clumsy. She had long legs and long arms. She never seemed to know where they were.

"Guess what?" Addy said to Noah and Zoe. "Miguel is announcing the winter musical on Monday. Do you want to try out?"

"No way," Noah laughed. "I'm not getting up on stage. But I'll help paint the set."

Miguel smiled. "I was hoping you would, Noah. You're The Club's best artist."

Addy looked at Zoe. "Well, you should definitely try out. You were great in last year's show."

Zoe considered. "Maybe. But it can't conflict with basketball. The winter season is just starting."

Miguel said, "We can probably work around that. Why don't you try out and see what happens?" He looked at Javi. "What about you, Javi? It would be great English practice."

Javi just shook his head. The whole idea was crazy. Singing American musical songs with his father was one thing. Performing them in front of an audience was another. He couldn't be in a musical where he could barely speak the language.

Still, part of him was excited. He'd never seen a musical. He'd only listened to his father's tapes. He looked forward to watching it.

I wonder which one it will be? Javi thought. Then he turned back to his books. He had a lot of work to do.

Chapter Three
Quetzals and Conquistadors

The apartment was quiet when Javi got home that night. As usual. His mother had left for her evening cleaning shift. His Uncle Eduardo still wasn't home from his construction job. Ana was sitting at the table staring into space. Her second-grade homework was in front of her. Abuelita was cooking something on the stove.

Back in Guatemala, Javi's grandmother had been the busy, bossy, beating heart of their family. She had survived so much. Her husband, Javi's grandfather, had died many years before Javi was born. He had been killed in the long civil war.

Abuelita had raised her sons by herself. She had been as strong and unshakable as a mountain.

Here, in America, Javi's grandma seemed like a faint echo of herself. She did everything she could, but this was not her world. She didn't know how to get to the supermarket. She didn't know how to use the laundry machine. She didn't know how to do a million other small things that Javi and Ana were learning to do for her. "I am so old to learn, my dears," she would say.

Javi washed up. He helped her fill three plates with a thick, spicy stew. *Pepian de pollo*, Javi thought. *That was always Papá's favorite*. Abuelita seemed to be thinking the same thing. She sighed heavily as she sat down. "*Buen provecho*," she said, gesturing to them to start eating.

They ate quietly. In the old days, dinner had

been very social. There were always extra places at the table. Friends would drop by and join them. Meals could take a long time. People told stories. Papá would get out his guitar. The evening would end with singing.

The silence pressed down on Javi. He wanted to fill it. "Abuelita," he said to his grandmother in Spanish. "Tell us a story."

His grandmother said, "I am too tired, Javi."

But Ana said, "Yes, please, Abuelita, tell us a story. Like you used to. Tell us about Tecún Umán."

Javi's grandma looked at Ana's thin, drawn face. Her granddaughter so rarely showed interest in anything these days.

"Very well, my children," she said. She

placed her hands flat on the table. "Our ancestors were a great people. They studied the stars. They made objects of great beauty. They built mighty cities. Tecún Umán was the last great ruler of that kingdom."

Abuelita paused.

"Then the conquistadors came," whispered Ana. She knew this story by heart.

Abuelita reached for her hand. "Yes, child. They came. They did not care about cities or stars or beauty. Their hearts were hard like iron. All they wanted was gold."

Javi's grandma had always loved to tell this tale. Her voice was growing stronger. Her face looked less tired.

Isn't it strange, Javi thought, *that even a sad story has that power?*

"Tecún Umán gathered a noble army," Abuelita continued. "A great band of warriors went out to meet the conquistadors. To fight for our land and our freedom."

"Don't forget the quetzal, Abuelita," said Javi.

His grandma smiled. "*Sí, Javito*. The quetzal is sacred to the Maya. Its long green feathers were worn in the headdresses of our kings. For ages, its song was the most beautiful of all the birds in the cloud forests."

"The quetzal was Tecún Umán's *nagual*, spirit guide. It flew over the battle, protecting him. For a while, the battle went well. Our warriors were brave. They loved their home. They were willing to risk everything."

Abuelita's voice fell. "But our people had never seen guns. They had never seen horses. They did not have armor or weapons made of metal. They could not win against these things for long."

Javi looked at Ana. Her eyes were wide even

though she knew what would happen.

"Finally, Tecún Umán came face-to-face with the captain of the conquistadors," Abuelita said. "They fought fiercely. Tecún Umán killed the conquistador's horse."

She closed her eyes. "But the conquistador rose from the ground. He took a spear and thrust it into Tecún Umán's heart. The battle was lost."

"Our stories say that when Tecún Umán fell, the quetzal was filled with grief. It came down from the sky. It settled on top of the warrior's lifeless body to mourn. When it rose, the feathers on its breast were stained red with blood. They have been red ever since. And the quetzal never sang its beautiful song again."

Ana said, "Never, Abuelita?"

Abuelita looked at her. "Never. It only croaks and calls. But the stories say the quetzal will sing once more if the land becomes truly free."

They were all quiet for a minute.

Then Javi said, "Will that ever happen, Abuelita?"

"I don't know, *mi amor*." His grandma's eyes grew dim. "There has been so much blood."

Javi lay awake in bed that night. He had his headphones on. He was listening to his father's music again. He thought of Tecún Umán. Of his grandfather. Of Papá. Of the beautiful quetzal.

Stained in blood. Silenced by sadness.

It was a long time before he fell asleep.

Chapter Four
The Secret

Monday morning, Javi said to Ana, "*Hermanita*, why don't you come to The Club today? I will ride on the bus with you all the way."

Ana looked scared. She shook her head.

Javi said, "You would love the art room. The teacher, Miss Hannah, is very kind. There is music. And there is a pool. We could learn to swim."

This just made Ana look more alarmed. Javi didn't say any more.

He wanted to help his sister overcome her

fear. But he knew he couldn't push too hard. She was afraid of the city bus. He couldn't make her believe it was safe. Not after what happened to Papá.

Javi got to The Club earlier than usual that afternoon. He didn't find any of his friends in the snack area. He ate his lunch quickly and went looking for Addy. He had math homework he didn't understand.

As he walked down the hallway, he heard music. It sounded like a violin. It was coming from the tutoring center. Javi smiled. It was probably Addy practicing. She was a good musician. She often used the tutoring center as a practice room when it was empty.

Javi stopped

outside the door to listen. Then he realized, with a sudden shock, that he recognized the music.

It was the opening song from *Fiddler on the Roof*. The part where the violin plays all alone.

Javi frowned. He knew this music by heart. Addy wasn't playing it quite right.

He walked in.

"No, Addy, no," Javi said. "It is playing like this." He sang the phrase so she could hear the rhythm.

Addy laid down her violin, looking surprised.

"Javi," Addy said slowly. "How do you know *Fiddler on the Roof*?"

Javi pulled out his cassette player. "My tapes," he said simply. "It's my…my…" he said, searching for the right word.

"Your favorite?" Addy suggested.

"Yes. My favorite," Javi answered.

"Well," Addy said. "It's the winter musical this year. Miguel just put up the posters."

Javi's face broke into a smile. "Good! Very good!" He would be able to see it with his mother and sister. Then Ana would see how great The Club was. She would start coming. And maybe that would help her light up again.

Addy picked up her violin. "I'm practicing for the tryouts. I want to be the fiddler." She grinned. "But Miguel probably won't let me up on a roof. I just got out of one leg cast. They'd be afraid I'd end up in another."

Javi laughed.

Addy said, "Sing that phrase again, Javi. I can't get it right."

He sang the phrase. Addy tried repeating it.

Javi shook his head. He sang it once more.

Addy said, "I think you know the music better than me." She tried the phrase again.

Javi started clapping. He wanted to help Addy keep the rhythm. Addy smiled and kept going. It was wonderful to hear someone play this piece again. Papá used to play it on the guitar. The whole family took turns singing.

Mamá loved to sing Yente's parts. Yente was the town gossip in the musical. She reminded Mamá of her Aunt Emilia. Ana sang the daughters' parts. She liked pretending she was in the wedding.

And Javi always did the main character, Tevye. He was a milkman struggling to make ends meet in a small Russian village. His little Jewish community was often threatened by the people living around them. Javi liked becoming someone so different from himself. Different, and yet oddly the same.

Javi had memorized big chunks of Tevye's part, English and all. He hadn't always known what he was saying. But he liked the sound of the big, rolling words.

Suddenly, Miguel appeared at the door. "What's going on?" he said, smiling.

Addy pointed at Javi. "Miguel!" Addy said. "Javi knows *Fiddler on the Roof*!"

Miguel turned to Javi. "Do you really?" he said.

Javi turned red. "No, no!" he said. "Only un poco…a little." He frowned at Addy. He did *not* want her to tell Miguel.

Addy seemed to understand. She laughed. "Javi was just helping me learn the first piece. He's got a good ear." She started talking about something else. "Are you going to direct the musical again, Miguel?"

"Yes, but your music teacher, Mr. Almadani, will handle all the songs. He's a much better musician than I am. We're lucky to have him here."

"I know," Addy said. "He's told me all about playing in the Syrian symphony.

Miguel left. Addy turned to Javi. "Admit it. You know the whole thing, don't you?"

Javi shrugged. He was embarrassed. "I am needing help with math," he said, changing the subject.

Addy looked at him for a long moment.

"Okay," she said, finally. "Let's take a look."

Addy explained the math problem to him. Soon, Javi was trying to complete the homework. Addy sat, watching him. She had a little smile on her face. She hummed a tune to herself. It was a snatch of a song from *Fiddler on the Roof*. She left it unfinished. Javi, not thinking, hummed the rest of the line.

Addy hummed another bit. Javi grinned this time. He finished the phrase. Addy grabbed her violin. She played the beginning of Tevye's song, "If I Were a Rich Man." Javi laughed and sang the first verse with her.

For a moment, he felt happier than he had in a long time.

"Javi!" Addy said, "You should try out for the musical! You sang all those English words! And you have a great voice."

Javi shook his head and clammed up again. Singing, in English, in front of all those people? It was a terrifying thought.

"No tell," he said to Addy. "No tell."

Addy looked at his pleading face.

"Okay," she said. "I promise not to tell."

But she didn't look happy about it.

Chapter Five
This Way and That Way

Javi avoided Addy that week. She kept pestering him. It wasn't that she broke her promise. She didn't tell anyone else Javi's secret. But she hadn't promised not to try to change his mind.

"Javi," she'd say any time they were alone. "You're a wonderful singer. And you know this musical better than anyone. You should try out!"

"No, Addy," Javi said.

"There are lots of small roles. People in the chorus. You wouldn't mind that, would you?"

"No, Addy," Javi repeated.

This conversation happened several times a day. Addy could be a determined talker.

Addy kept trying to make her point. On Tuesday, they were sitting with Milo in the snack area. Addy kept humming little bits of the Fiddler music. But she kept making mistakes. On purpose. She knew it would drive Javi crazy. He'd want to correct her. But Javi gripped his pencil tighter and kept to his work.

On Wednesday, Addy and Javi were in the tutoring room when Zoe walked in. She'd decided to try out. Miguel had told everyone he would use a scene between Tevye and his wife, Golde, for the audition. Zoe wanted Addy to help her rehearse.

"Wow, Zoe, I'm really busy," Addy said. "I'm studying for a test. But I'm sure Javi could help you. It's good language practice."

Javi glared at Addy. She was *not* studying

for a test. But in the end he read the lines. First, because Zoe had said, "Would you, Javi?" And second because…well…because Zoe was *muy bonita*, very pretty. He didn't want to say no.

In the end, he had to admit that it was a lot of fun. Zoe was very good as Golde.

"Wow, Javi," Zoe said. "You were great! You should try out."

Addy just looked smug.

That night, all the adults were home for dinner. This was a special treat. Abuelita made *kak-ik*. Grandma had been famous for her turkey stew in their hometown.

Mamá didn't smile often now. Javi

was happy to see the lines fade a little from her face as she sat at the table. Ana pressed up close beside her. Javi knew how much his sister missed her mother after school.

But Mamá needed to work. She was trying to be strong. Like Abuelita had been strong. She was determined to support her family. They couldn't rely on Uncle Eduardo for everything.

Javi glanced at his uncle. He had never met him before they came to America. He looked so much like his brother. A grayer, more serious version of Papá. It still gave Javi a little shock sometimes. So alike, and so different.

Uncle Eduardo had come to the United States a few years after Javi's grandfather died. He was the oldest son. Though he was only sixteen, he wanted to support his family. He worked very hard. He found a good job in construction. Soon, he made enough money to send some home.

Years passed. Papá and Mamá got married. In his letters, Uncle Eduardo urged Papá to bring his family to America. He could give them a good life there.

Papá had always said, "Not yet." He thought Guatemala gave them a good life already. He loved his country. He loved his town. He had a decent job as a bus driver. Things were not so bad.

Then the gangs arrived. They threatened people who would not pay them money. Javi's father and mother talked about leaving.

Too late.

The money Uncle Eduardo sent for their tickets arrived the day after the funeral.

The only thing Javi had ever heard Uncle Eduardo say about it was, "My brother had his head in the clouds. If he had listened to me, he would be alive today."

Javi was still angry about that.

As they finished their meal, Uncle Eduardo started asking Javi and Ana about school. He did this whenever he saw them. "You must work very hard," he was saying to them in Spanish. "Like I did."

Ana was looking at the ground and nodding. Javi knew she was a little afraid of Uncle Eduardo. He was so stern.

Without knowing why he said it, Javi interrupted. "They are putting on a musical at The Club. It is *Fiddler on the Roof.* Anyone who wants to can try out."

Everyone looked at him, surprised.

"Oh," said Mamá, "How wonderful! That was one of your Papá's favorites."

Uncle Eduardo grunted. "Music," he said. "That's all my brother ever cared about. He was too busy singing to see what was happening around him." He looked at Javi. "Are you thinking of trying out?"

Javi dropped his eyes. He tried to hide the anger in his voice. "No, Uncle," he said. At least, he hadn't been thinking of it much. Not until that very moment.

"But," said Grandma, firmly, looking at Ana's face. "We can go see it, Eduardo. You used to love the music as much as your brother did. Who sent him all the tapes?"

Javi looked up. He had not known that.

"Well," said Uncle Eduardo gruffly, "that was years ago. I was young."

He turned to Javi. "Concentrate on schoolwork. On learning English."

Uncle Eduardo's eyes looked suddenly sad.

"Your family is depending on you," he said. "You are the oldest son."

Late that night, Javi got up to get a glass of water. He thought everyone was asleep. He tiptoed down the hallway. Then he froze. There was a light on in the kitchen.

His uncle was sitting at the table. There was a pile of papers in front of him. It looked like he was reading old letters.

Javi could recognize the handwriting even from the darkness of the hallway.

It was Papá's.

While Javi watched, Uncle Eduardo covered his face. Javi thought he heard a soft sob.

Javi turned around. He slipped back down the hallway to his room.

He was careful not to make a sound.

Chapter Six
The Audition

All Thursday during school, Javi debated with himself. Should he audition? He hadn't even considered it at first. But singing with Addy. Acting with Zoe. It had woken up something inside of him. Something that he had thought he would never feel again.

But there was Uncle Eduardo. Javi couldn't figure out him out. When he had talked about Javi's Papá last night, Javi had wanted to punch him. But that moment in the kitchen. The tapes. How hard Javi knew he worked to help his family. It was confusing.

And Uncle Eduardo hadn't really forbidden him to audition. He had just said to work hard in school and learn English. Well, Javi was working hard. Very hard. His grades were good. And being in the musical would probably *help* him learn English.

Then again, being in the musical meant standing in front of a lot of people and *speaking* English. He'd been trying to avoid that for four months.

Of course, it would only be a small part. A nameless villager, or a minor role like Avram, the bookseller. That wouldn't be too bad. Standing in the back, singing in the chorus.

He went back and forth, all day. And half the night.

Then it was Friday.

When he got to The Club, he walked straight past the snack area. He didn't want to talk to anyone. He was too nervous.

He went to the auditorium. Miguel and Mr. Almadani were on stage, setting up chairs and a table near a piano. There were some other kids there already. Addy was sitting in the front row, holding her violin. He sat down next to her. "Do not be saying a thing," Javi said.

"You mean *don't say anything*," Addy said. She grinned.

More kids started arriving. Miguel and Mr. Almadani sat down behind the table. They started calling groups of kids up on stage. Javi was growing more and more nervous. He thought about changing his mind.

"Hey, guys!" Zoe appeared beside them. She was still wearing her basketball uniform. "I just got out of practice. Have you gone yet?"

"Not yet," said Addy. "There are a lot of kids trying out."

Just then, Miguel called up the three kids who were auditioning for the fiddler. Javi thought that Addy was easily the best of them all. She would get the part for sure.

Zoe leaned over and said, "I hope we get to go up together."

Javi nodded, feeling a little sick. He'd have to go through with it now. He couldn't back out in front of Zoe.

Miguel called their names. They read the scene for him. Javi knew he got a lot of the words wrong, but he didn't care. He wasn't going to get a speaking part anyway.

Then Mr. Almadani took over. Javi didn't know him well. He was a slight, balding man who smiled kindly at them over his glasses. He spoke

with a clear, though foreign, accent. Javi hoped he could sound like that in English one day.

Mr. Almadani had the group run through some scales. Then he asked each kid to sing a phrase he played on the piano. Some kids did this a little more and some a little less. Javi couldn't really tell why. Mr. Almadani nodded the same way at each kid. He said, "Yes, thank you," after each one sang. When it was his turn, Mr. Almadani made Javi sing more than anyone else.

Zoe and Javi walked up the aisle together when they were done. "You sounded really good, Javi," Zoe said. "I'm sure you'll get in." She sighed. "And now we wait. They are putting up the cast list on Monday."

Javi felt his nervousness draining away. He wasn't thinking much about Monday. He had made it through auditions. It hadn't been too bad. That felt like a win by itself.

Javi decided he should break the news to his uncle. He couldn't hide the fact if he ended up going to practice. Better sooner than later.

They were in the kitchen together Saturday morning. "Uncle Eduardo," Javi said in Spanish. "I auditioned for the musical."

His uncle frowned.

"My Club director told me to," Javi said quickly. "He thought it would be good for my English." This was kind of true. And Javi knew it would impress his uncle. People didn't question teachers where they came from.

"I won't have a big part," Javi added. "I'll be able to get all my work done. I promise."

His uncle grunted. He muttered something about "waste of time." But he didn't say anything else.

Javi left the kitchen. The worst was over. He smiled. Now he could enjoy himself. He was looking forward to singing with the chorus.

On Monday, Javi walked down to the auditorium entrance to see the cast list.

There was a little cluster of kids standing there. Addy and Zoe were with them. Addy spotted him. "Javi!" she said urgently. "Come look!"

Javi scanned the list. Zoe was Golde. Addy was the Fiddler. He finally found his name. He wasn't in the chorus. He wasn't even Avram.

He was Tevye.

Chapter Seven
Wonder of Wonders

Javi turned pale. His friends were congratulating him. He walked away without responding. He felt sick to his stomach. He couldn't be Tevye. He couldn't. What would he tell his family? What were Miguel and Mr. Almadani thinking?

He found them in the auditorium, talking about set design.

"Here's our star!" Miguel said, smiling. "Congratulations, Javi!"

Javi shook his head. "No," he said urgently. "No. This is mistake. I cannot speak all the words."

Mr. Almadani said, "Of course you can. You've memorized every song already. And you have such a voice!"

"And your scene with Zoe was wonderful!" said Miguel. "We'll help you with pronunciation. But you already have the character. You were Tevye when you did that scene. Have you done theater before?"

"No," Javi said. "I am not knowing these things."

"We'll help you," said Miguel. "Don't worry."

Mr. Almadani looked over his glasses at Javi. "Did you know that the most famous person to ever play Tevye didn't know English either? He was from Israel. He only knew the musical in Hebrew. He memorized the Broadway album." He smiled. "You've already done that!"

Javi still looked panicked.

"Javi," Miguel said. "Let's make a deal. You rehearse as Tevye for three days. If you still feel the same after that, I'll cast someone else."

Javi looked at Miguel. He looked at Mr. Almadani. He took a long breath. "Okay," he said. "Okay. Just three days."

But three days later, neither Miguel nor Mr. Almadani bothered asking Javi what his choice was. It was obvious.

Riding home from the first day of rehearsal, Javi felt like someone had flipped a switch on inside him.

It wasn't that being Tevye was easy. It was really, really hard. Stage directions were confusing.

The dances were complicated. Speaking was difficult. He had to concentrate to pronounce words clearly. But the minute Mr. Almadani started playing Tevye's music, all Javi's fears fell away.

It felt like coming home.

Miguel and Mr. Almadani were patient teachers. They knew lots of kids hadn't been in a musical before. But they drew the best out of them. Javi liked to watch them when he wasn't acting. He wondered if he could have a job like theirs someday.

One day, Miguel said to the cast, "You have all worked really hard. You know your lines and music. Now I want you to bring these characters to life."

He paused. "This musical can be sad. Some pretty awful things happen to these people. That means we need to make the happy parts very, very joyful. Your homework tonight is to ask yourself, what's the best thing that ever happened to me? What's your wonder of wonders, as one of our songs says? I want to see that joy on our stage."

Javi thought about the question all the way home. He didn't want to answer it. Answering meant remembering. He had been trying so hard to avoid that. Remembering was painful. Remembering meant thinking of Papá.

Javi fought the question all evening. But late that night, in the darkness of his room, he gave in. It was like he opened a door. He let the memories come flooding back. And he knew what his answer would be.

It had happened three months before Papá died. He woke Javi in the middle of the night. Bad things were already happening in their town. Javi had sat up in alarm.

But his father just wanted to take him up into the cloud forest.

They reached a clearing a little before dawn. "My father," said Papá, "used to bring Eduardo and me up here. We always kept it secret. I wanted to show you in case…" He didn't finish the sentence.

The forest was full of noises. The animals were waking up. Javi and his father sat on a rotten log. Javi started to feel cold. He fidgeted. "Be still," Papá whispered. "And watch. We might be lucky."

Suddenly, there was a commotion. Something burst above the trees. A large bird spiraled up into the sky with a rough-sounding croak. Its blood-red breast caught the light of the rising sun. It flashed like fire. The bird's impossibly long, green tail feathers trailed behind it. They looked like blazing emerald streamers.

It was a quetzal.

The bird soared up until it was a speck in the sky. Then it turned. It dove with heart-stopping speed straight back down into the canopy.

Another bird exploded from the trees. It made the same breathtaking arc through the sky. Another bird followed, and then another, and another. Their long, flowing tails made them look like flying, feathered snakes.

The display finally ended. The noise ended. Javi took a deep, shuddering breath. He turned to look at his father. There were tears running down Papá's face.

"Remember," Papá had said. "Remember the beauty, Javi."

He put a hand on Javi's head.

"No matter what else happens, today we are blessed."

Chapter Eight
Darkness

The next few weeks flew by in a whirlwind of rehearsals and schoolwork. Every day, Javi put off telling his family about his part. He didn't want to risk breaking the spell. The musical was coming together.

Javi's songs were great. His spoken lines were good. There were only a few places where he still felt shaky. And his scenes with Zoe were making everyone laugh.

Most of all, Javi loved being Tevye. He loved

feeling his joy, his sadness, his loss, his love. Javi was pouring all his own feelings into the character. He knew Tevye wasn't real, but it felt like if they met, they would understand each other.

Noah and Miss Hannah, the art teacher, led a team of students that was building the sets. Little village houses were painted on a backdrop. The

front of Tevye's cottage was hammered together out of wood. Miguel had designed a clever platform for the top. It let Addy "stand" on the roof without risk of falling. Well, without much risk of falling.

Milo started practicing the stage lights. It was amazing what a difference they made. When they were on, the auditorium disappeared. It made the stage world seem so real.

So did the costumes. Miguel had borrowed a whole cast's worth of them from a nearby high school. They were a little big. The boys were having a hard time with the beards. The girls were tripping over their skirts. Still, if you squinted, you could believe you were in an old Russian village.

The final week arrived. The show was Saturday. They had been practicing their scenes separately. It was time to start stringing them together.

By Wednesday, they were nearly through the first act. There was one final scene. Javi knew what was going to happen. He had practiced it before. The joyful wedding celebration of Tevye's daughter would be broken up by an angry mob.

What Javi hadn't realized was how different the scene would feel with the lights, the set, and the costumes. It was all horribly real and lifelike. The figures in the doorway were not kids anymore. They were angry, powerful men. They were holding clubs and threatening violence, or worse.

When Javi saw them, he froze. He knew he had a line, but he couldn't speak. He couldn't breathe. There was a strange rushing sound in his ears. He felt an overwhelming need to escape.

He jumped off the stage, ran up the aisle, and crashed through the doors into the hallway. He felt dizzy. His breath was coming in short, frantic gasps. He tore off his beard. He couldn't stop shaking.

Javi slumped against the wall. *What's wrong with me?* He pressed the heels of his hands into his eyes. He wanted to block the images in his head. The gang. His father. The bus. *No!* Javi thought. *It's just a musical.*

He heard the doors open. Someone knelt

down beside him. It was Mr. Almadani. "Javi?" he said. "Are you all right?"

Javi couldn't answer. His mind was reeling. *They had clubs. It isn't the same.*

No, in Javi's story, they had come with guns. Men with hearts like iron.

More people were around him now. Noah and Addy. Zoe and Milo. They all looked frightened.

Miguel arrived. Mr. Almadani said, "I think he's having a panic attack."

He took Javi by the hand. "Javi," Mr. Almadani said gently. "You're safe. Breathe deep. Tell me what's wrong."

"My father," Javi whispered. "They came for Papá. Men like that."

Miguel looked around. "OK, guys. Let's give Javi some space." He led them back into the auditorium.

Javi tried to control his breath. Mr. Almadani squeezed his hand tighter. "Tell me, Javi. Tell me the story."

Javi looked up into Mr. Almadani's face. There was something in his eyes. Something that understood.

Javi's story spilled out in broken, halting English.

His father had worked for a bus company. It was a good job. Then the gangs arrived. They told the owner that he had to pay them money. For "protection." The owner had refused.

The gang beat up some bus drivers, including Javi's father. The owner agreed to pay. Javi's father kept working. There were no other jobs. But he started planning to leave Guatemala. To join his brother in America.

Meanwhile, the owner ran out of money. The gang had taken it all. They didn't believe him.

So they went after the bus drivers again. This time with guns…

Javi couldn't finish. Mr. Almadani looked grim. He nodded. He was gripping Javi's hand so tightly that it hurt. But somehow, Javi felt a little bit better. Like a weight had lifted. He could breathe again.

For a long moment, neither of them spoke.

Then Javi said, "The musical…Mr. Almadani, I can't…"

Mr. Almadani spoke very quietly. "Listen, Javi. I know. They came for me, too. In Syria. They beat me. They broke my arm. I thought I'd never play again. And they destroyed my beautiful city. It's all gone. There is nothing left for me to go back to."

He sighed. "But I have to tell the story. We have to tell our stories. All the stories. Tevye's story. Otherwise, they win."

Mr. Almadani helped Javi up.

"Go home, now. Get some rest." He put a hand on Javi's shoulder. "You decide. Miguel can always take your part. But you would make a better Tevye."

Javi shook his head. "Why?" he said.

"Don't you know?" said Mr. Almadani. "Because you *are* Tevye." He went back in the auditorium.

Javi was left standing in the hallway, thinking about everything that meant.

Chapter Nine
The Song

The only person in the house when Javi got home was his mother. She was pulling a cake out of the oven. *Bocado de Reina*. Javi's favorite dessert.

"Where is everybody?" Javi said in Spanish.

"I sent your uncle out for groceries with Grandma and Ana," Mamá replied.

There was a silence.

"Did Miguel call you?" Javi asked.

"*Sí.* Sit down." She gave him a slice of cake and a cup of hot coffee. She got one for herself and sat down beside him.

"You know about the musical then. About me playing Tevye."

"I know," Mamá said. She took a sip of coffee.

"And?" Javi said.

"And I am very proud of you. Your father would be, too."

Javi dropped his head in his hands. The tears began to well up. "Did Miguel tell you what happened?"

"He did. Eat your cake, Javito. And your coffee. Don't let it get cold."

Javi took a bite of cake. A sip of coffee. He still felt shaky. But he was glad to sit here, alone, next to his mother. He could feel her presence with his eyes closed, like the sun.

He whispered, "I don't think I can do it, Mamá. I don't think I can do the musical."

"Why not, *mi corazón*?"

"You remember the scene at the end of the wedding?" Javi said. He covered his face. "The memories came back so clearly. Of Papá. How can I sing again after what happened to him? What happened to all of us? It is like the quetzal."

He heard the click of a coffee cup coming down on the table.

"It is *not* like the quetzal," his mother said sharply.

Javi opened his eyes. He looked at his mother, surprised. She was so patient. So gentle. But there was something urgent in her face now.

"Why do you think Abuelita has stayed so strong? Or why your Papá kept that job? Or why your uncle and I work so hard?" Mamá touched his arm. "It is for you. For you and Ana."

Mamá looked almost fierce now. "The legend of the quetzal is part of our story. As a people. But it must not be *your* story, Javi. You must sing again. You and Ana must both sing again."

She took a deep breath. "We will be at the musical on Saturday. All of us. Even your uncle. I will make sure."

She held his face in her hands. There were tears in her eyes. "And Javi, sweet Javito, remember. Your father will be there, too."

It was hard going back to The Club the next day. Javi knew they were all talking about him.

They must be.

His friends did their best. Zoe and Addy both gave him a hug. Noah asked him a question about Guatemalan art. And Milo showed him a new bug. He'd found it dead in one of the lights. He still wasn't sure what it was.

They were trying to make things feel normal. Javi was grateful.

Rehearsal was okay. Javi asked Miguel to start with the last scene in Act One. But could they leave the lights up?

He kept his mind shut tight. He got through it fine.

On Friday, he did the scene with the lights down. He got through the whole show. Again, it was fine. But something was missing. Tevye was not there with him. He wasn't sure what to do.

He went to see Mr. Almadani.

"Yes, I noticed," he said, answering Javi's

question. "You've shut a door."

"But how can I…how do you…?" His English words failed him. *How do you survive if you let all the memories in?*

Mr. Almadani smiled sadly. "I remember an evening a long time ago, Javi. A garden full of stars in my hometown, Aleppo. The air was filled with the scent of jasmine. It was the night I met my wife, Zaina. I remember it now and know I was blessed."

Javi stared at him. Then he nodded. "Thank you, Mr. Almadani."

On Saturday, Javi looked out in the audience before the show. Uncle Eduardo, Abuelita, Ana, and Mamá were sitting just a few rows back. Ana was looking around. She looked nervous, but excited. Uncle Eduardo was reading the program. He pointed at something and began talking quickly to Abuelita. Javi saw Mamá smile. She hadn't told them.

Miguel called for places. The opening music began. His new friend, Addy, in this strange new place, was playing it on her violin. His family was dancing and singing to it on a warm summer evening. The same music. He opened the door to it all. He stepped into the spotlight.

Tevye came with him.

And so did his Papá.

The show went well. A few beards fell off. Addy nearly tumbled off the roof. Golde came in late once and Tevye had to make lines up. In English. But the show went very, very well. The village danced with joy. The audience roared with laughter. The people left their home, Anatevka, to find a new life. There wasn't a dry eye in the house.

Javi and his friends came out to take their bow. Milo brought up the house lights. Javi looked out at the audience. His Uncle Eduardo was weeping. His mother and Abuelita were laughing. And the eyes of Ana, little Ana, were shining like stars.

It's strange, Javi thought. *How powerful a story is. Even a sad one.*

He looked at the people on stage. At Addy. Zoe. Noah and Milo. Miguel. And Mr. Almadani.

His heart was full. He'd found a home.

Tonight, no matter what else happens, I am blessed.

In his imagination, a quetzal rose, spiraling up through the air. Its tail feathers gleamed and danced in the rising sun. And this time, it was singing.

Want to Keep Reading?

Turn the page for a sneak peek at
the next book in the series.

ISBN: 9781538382431

Chapter One
Hurricane Addy

Addy's Monday began with a smash.

It happened in first period Biology. Addy was late. She hurried to her lab table. She swung her backpack onto the desk. The backpack knocked against a cart. A rolling cart full of glass jars.

Crash! Crash! Crash! Three jars tipped off the cart. They smashed on the floor. Pale, flabby lab specimens slid across the tile. A strong, sharp smell filled the air. Her classmates screamed.

"Clear the room!" shouted her teacher. Gagging, Addy said, "I'm so sorry, Ms. Park! Can I help you clean…?"

"No," said Ms. Park firmly. She threw open all the windows. "Thank you, Addy. But *please* don't help."

The kids gathered in the hallway. A boy laughed. "Hurricane Addy strikes again!"

Hurricane Addy.

Again.

The name had followed Addy for a long time. Ever since she'd tried out for the school's field hockey team. In just 10 minutes, she'd sent not one but two teammates to the nurse's office. The coach took her stick away. He suggested that she might like volleyball.

Addy thought that could be a good idea. She had grown three inches over the summer. She towered over her classmates. Volleyball was supposed to be a good sport for tall kids.

The volleyball coach was excited about her height. She put Addy in the center of the front row. "You'll make a great middle blocker," she said.

Addy lasted a little longer at this tryout. But other players kept missing the ball. They were too busy avoiding Addy's long arms and legs.

"Addy!" the coach called. "Stop spinning around like a hurricane!"

Addy tried. But she wasn't sure where her legs and arms were. They'd grown so quickly. Sometimes, they seemed like they belonged to someone else.

The more embarrassed Addy felt, the more clumsy she got. As she stumbled off the court, she heard the coach say, "She looks like a baby giraffe on ice."

She didn't make the team.

In fact, she hadn't made any team. And

she'd tried out for most of them. And the name Hurricane had stuck. She had laughed about it at first. Nobody was trying to be mean. But she hadn't thought the nickname would last. It was starting to annoy her.

ABOUT
the
AUTHOR

Elizabeth Gordon has a master's degree in Children's Literature from Hollins University. She was a finalist for the Hunger Mountain Katherine Paterson Prize for Young Adult and Children's Writing, the winner of the Hollins University Houghton Mifflin Harcourt Scholarship, and winner of the SCBWI Barbara Karlin Grant. She has published nine middle grade books so far, including a five-book superhero series.

Check out more books at:
www.west44books.com

An imprint of Enslow Publishing

WEST **44** BOOKS™